The Fan...
Mash-Up Machines

Tyler Byrd
and
N.S. Blackman

Text copyright © 2023
Illustrations copyright © 2023
Dinosaur Books Ltd

All Rights Reserved
Published by Dinosaur Books Ltd, London
www.dinosaurbooks.co.uk

The right of Tyler Byrd and N.S. Blackman to be
identified as the authors of this work has been
asserted by them in accordance with the
Copyright, Designs and Patents Act, 1988

ISBN 978-0-9927525-4-5
British Library Cataloguing in Publication Data
A CIP catalogue record for this book is available from
the British Library

Visit www.dinosaurbooks.co.uk
for all the latest Mash-Up Machines news

Editor
Sonya McGilchrist

Authors
N.S. Blackman
Ty Byrd

Illustrators
Vicky Fieldhouse
Natalie Cooper
N.S. Blackman

The Mash-Up Championship

The next race
is about to begin!

Teams competing in this race:

1. Zonka Speedkings
2. Acceligator
3. Team Dragg
4. Lightspeed XTC
5. Mister Crank
6. Fizz-Bang Crew
7. Team Trakstar
8. Curlew Capri
9. Team Hippo
10. Svenja Masher
11. Hakondi Hackers
12. Wild Wicked Duo
13. The Overtakers
14. High Tech Mike
15. Araknikid 865
16. Oldster Boldster
17. Wagon Wheelies
18. Flash & Dash
19. Team Gushmore
20. Blackbird Attack
21. Sliding Penguin
22. Hyper-loopy-doopy
23. HGV Holiday
24. Dragon-Wagon
25. A Car too Far
26. Racing Demons
27. Rebel Racers
28. Faster than You
29. Here to Win
30. Red Eye Riders

Map by N.S.Blackman

Welcome!

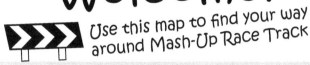

Use this map to find your way around Mash-Up Race Track

Underground pipes bring thermal energy from volcano

Mash Island

To the desert

Emergency Rescuers' centre

Renewable energy plant

Team camp site

Test Track

News room

Drone launchpad

Mash HQ

Workshop

Recycling

Refreshments

East Stand

Visitor entrance

Just a little bit before the start

The Mash-Up teams were gathering.

Some came to the island by boat. Some flew in by helicopter.

And two of them – just to prove how daring they were – dived into the sea from a hot air balloon and swam. Still wearing their crash helmets they walked up the beach dripping and waving to the crowds.

But whoever they were, and however they arrived, all the teams found exactly the same thing waiting for them on the island.

A letter from Mr Murcan.

The Mash-Up Machines Challenge

Dear racers,

Welcome to the world's most **wild** and **thrilling** race competition.

Teams from around the world are competing to be crowned this year's

Mash-Up Champs!

Is this your first time here?
Here's what you need to know...

Remember, **this is not like any other race track.**

Ordinary cars are **not** allowed, only Mash-Up Machines, invented from scraps and spares.

Is your machine the best? Let's find out...

You will be driving into the **strangest** places – including canyons, waterfalls, tunnels, loops, dips, ramps, jumps, bridges and bumps.

Beware! **At any moment** there may be a **trap** waiting for you. All the traps are totally safe (probably). But accidents can happen, so remember to wear your crash helmets and fire-proof costumes at all times.

Any questions, come and see me. Good luck. You will need it.

Yours ever-so-kindly,
Mr Murcan,
Chief Planner

PS. Do not try to cheat! You will be **Caught.**

After they had read their letters, the drivers and navigators went to the camp site where they would be staying. They had just two days to relax and get ready.

Nearby, in the workshops, the inventors and fixers were busy making final checks on the mash-up machines…

Chapter One

Jace leaned against his broom and stared at the hippopotamus.

He was supposed to be sweeping the floor, getting it spotless. But the picture

of the hippo was
impossible to ignore.
The creature – so cheerful,
with a hat and sunglasses – was
printed onto the side of the most
magical mash-up machine that Jace had
ever seen. A little blue racer with round
headlights.

Jace pushed the broom again (scooping up
a sweet wrapper) and edged closer.

Now he could see a name painted on the
vehicle in small
gold letters.
"Dexybel".
There was
something

extra special about the racer, with its cool
curves and neat tail-fin. Jace stared at it,
wondering how fast it could go.

A drone zipped overhead, carrying a

Meet the Fixers!

Mash-Up Fixers are experts with machines. They can make or mend anything on wheels!

Tool Case

Mash-Up Fixer

Mash-Up kit changes depending on the job

Bodywork specialist

Power tools are essential for metal bashing and heavy-duty repairs

Crush-proof boots protect feet and toes

spare machine part to a waiting mash-up fixer. Another drone buzzed back in the opposite direction. Below, a trolley rolled

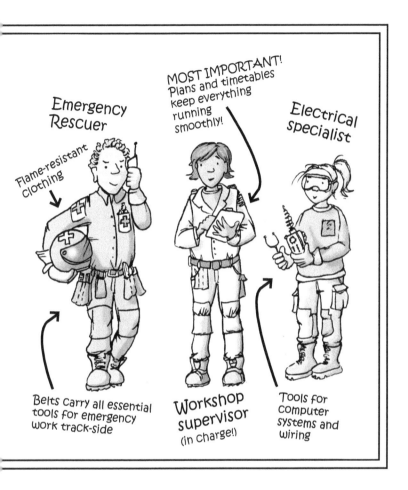

Emergency
Rescuer

MOST IMPORTANT!
Plans and timetables
keep everything
running
smoothly!

Electrical
specialist

Flame-resistant
clothing

Belts carry all essential
tools for emergency
work track-side

Workshop
supervisor
(in charge!)

Tools for
computer
systems and
wiring

past, delivering tools.

All around, in every corner of the

workshop, teams of people were fixing

machines together. Time was short. The
first race would be starting soon – and every
vehicle was being worked on.

But for some reason, no one was paying
any attention to the Dexybel.

"Why is nobody checking you, then?"

Jace whispered to the bright blue racer.

It was covered in dents and scratches. Jace could see that it wasn't as smart as any of the other vehicles. But he knew one thing for certain, even if nobody else did: the Dexybel was the coolest thing on four wheels.

"Team Hippo!" declared the fat, cheerful letters around the picture of the

hippopotamus:

> *"I'm big and I'm grey –*
> *Get outta my way!"*

Jace laughed.

"Get outta my way…"

He leaned closer, peering through the driver's window at the dashboard controls.

Interesting…

Then, without warning, a voice boomed out across the workshop and made Jace jump.

Mr Murcan was back!

Jace snatched up his broom and began sweeping.

Mr Murcan was the race track manager and chief obstacle planner. Jace had never seen him smile.

And he wasn't smiling now. He was growling at some unlucky person near the door.

"Two days! That's all you've got until the first race – no daydreaming!"

Then he came striding across the workshop with his hands clamped behind his back, and his eyes scanning from side to side.

Mr Murcan had the sort of eyes that saw everything.

As he came nearer (pacing and scanning) all the crews suddenly looked extra busy working on their machines.

Jace quickly made himself busy too. He whistled as he pushed his broom along at double speed.

Mr Murcan folded his arms and looked around the bright, clean workshop. He nodded, satisfied, and seemed about to leave.

But then he stopped.

"Hmph!"

He looked straight at Jace and beckoned

with one finger.

"M…me?" blinked Jace.

Mr Murcan nodded. And he pointed to something on the floor, over by the door.

Jace looked – he could just about see what it was: a tiny piece of metal no bigger than a button.

"Oops, sorry," said Jace, hurrying over with his broom to sweep it up.

But Mr Murcan didn't reply.

He was pacing away already, off to inspect another part of the race track.

The Mash-Up Machines Challenge was the most exciting racing competition in the world.

Like every other young person on Rumblemore Island Jace had always dreamed of visiting the workshops, and looking round the track.

But he never really thought it would happen.

But then he got lucky – incredibly lucky – and all because of his mum.

Mrs Tanna worked at the café near the track. She made sandwiches and pies.

And one morning, when she was collecting plates from the tables, she overheard a customer talking on the phone.

"Yes, yes…we really need another helper in the workshop…just for the summer. But I've looked everywhere and I can't find anyone suitable…"

The customer was Maya, the woman in charge of the Mash-Up Machines workshop.

"Er – excuse me," said Mrs Tanna, (after Maya had finished her phone call). "Excuse me, but I know a boy who's very hard working…and he loves machines…"

Which his how Jace came to be here right now, in the middle of the action, with these amazing Mash-Up racers all around him.

He knew how incredibly lucky he was, even if he did spend most of his time cleaning floors and making cups of tea for people.

Jace gazed dreamily at the Dexybel again – such a cool, cool invention – a bright blue wonder, just waiting for someone to…

Then a hand clamped down on his shoulder and Jace dropped the broom.

The hand belonged to Maya. And Maya's face was just behind it, smiling.

"OK?"

Jace gulped, and did his best to smile back.

"Yes – er, I mean great…"

"Good! Follow me, quick. We've got a problem…"

And Maya was off, striding up the stairs to her office, two at a time.

Problem? What did Maya mean?

As Jace
climbed the metal
stairs, his heart
was racing.

Maya was a
very important

29

person. She was the Mash-Up chief technical officer – the top machines expert – and of course she was in charge of all the fixers.

She was always cheerful. From Jace's first day Maya had called him 'J' and made him feel welcome.

But as Jace climbed the stairs he couldn't help wondering…

What did Maya mean: "we've got a problem"?

Maybe…maybe he was about to be told that his time at the workshop was over. Yes…that must be it…

The thought of leaving and becoming just an ordinary 12-year-old at home in the holidays, instead of the island's youngest Mash-Up helper, made his stomach knot with dread.

"In here," said Maya, ducking through the door.

Maya's office was a shiny glass box on stilts, with a spiral staircase that twisted up, winding round and round, through an opening in the floor. From here, she had a perfect view over the workshop below.

Maya kept everything in her office spotless. Her tools were stacked on shelves behind the door, and her laptop was always charging.

On a whiteboard, behind her desk, she'd written a list of all the Mash-Up machines in the race. And next to each one was written the name of the fixer in charge.

Maya saw Jace gazing around at all the tools, and she smiled.

"You know what, J? I keep the most important things in this drawer here."

She was pointing to her desk. "Top secret. Can you guess what they are?"

Jace shook his head – and Maya pulled out a paper bag.

"My sandwiches. Made by your mum," she smiled. And she tossed one over to Jace. "Cheese and tomato today."

Jace laughed.

"Thanks."

The two of them stood there, eating for a moment. Then Maya looked more serious.

"I saw you looking at Team Hippo's

racer," she said, sitting down on the edge of her desk.

"Yes, but I was just…I mean, I didn't touch anything…" Jace stuttered.

"Don't worry, you're not in trouble," laughed Maya. "I love the Dexybel too."

She looked down at the workshop, where the Team Hippo car was sitting, ignored among all the activity.

The Dexy had several large dents. And pasted on the windscreen was a piece of cardboard with big letters written on it: NO BRAKES. This was to warn people that the car couldn't stop – not that it mattered much, because it couldn't go either. The only way of getting the Dexybel to move was to push it.

"The trouble is, there's no one to fix it," sighed Maya. "Team Hippo haven't got much money, I'm afraid. And now their fixer has gone missing. We've only got two days until the race and I haven't got anyone to spare."

"Missing? Where did the fixer go?"

Maya shrugged and shook her head.

"Nobody seems to know."

Then she looked at Jace.

"So, what about *you*? Do you want the job?"

"What?"

"Fix that car. The Dexybel."

"You mean…*me*?" gasped Jace, not quite believing what he was hearing.

"Well you're the only other person here," Maya laughed. "And I'm not talking to myself. Come on!"

Then she sprinted off down the spiral stairs with Jace clattering behind, trying to keep up.

"Your mum said you were good at inventing things. So you've got two days. 48 hours," Maya called over her shoulder. "Repair the Dexybel, then you can become a Mash-Up Machines fixer – a full member of my crew."

Chapter Two

Five minutes later Jace was standing in front of the Dexybel, pulling on a pair of protective gloves and trying to remember everything he knew about repairing machines.

His hands were shaking.

"Keep calm…"

Close to, he could see
how beaten-up the Dexybel
was.

"Don't worry, we'll soon fix
you…"

He patted the hippo logo.

He wanted the machine to know that he
was the right person to fix it.

He wanted to believe that himself.

"Here goes…"

He took a deep breath and reached out to
lift the bonnet…

But suddenly Jace heard a strange
thumping sound.

"Get in there! Blast you! Get in!"

Somebody was shouting.

Jace twisted round – and over by the door he saw the most extraordinary sight.

A man was trying to stuff a black plastic bag into one of the rubbish trolley bins – but the bin kept rolling away from him!

*"Recycling only...Recycling only...*a robotic voice kept repeating.

The man ignored the instruction, and  kept chasing behind the trolley bin trying to cram the bag into it.

"Take it, you stupid thing! Take it!"

"It's OK, there's another bin over there," called Jace, hurrying over to help. "This one is for recycling only."

Jace pointed towards the dumpster where general waste was supposed to go. But the man just glared at him.

Jace tried to explain.

"The bins won't take the wrong type of rubbish, sorry. They're computer controlled – see the little tablet attached at the back? It's screening your rubbish."

Recycling only... Recycling only...

"I haven't got time for that. And I'm not arguing with a stupid computer!"

The man gave the bin

40

(and the tablet) a kick.

"Don't you realise who I am?" he growled

at the tablet. "I'm Deesol Dragg, the famous racing driver."

His face twitched ominously.

"Recycling only..." the tablet replied. *"Stand clear. Bin reversing..."*

The man was about to kick the screen again, even harder, but suddenly he stopped and looked at Jace. He had noticed the Dexybel.

"What a horrible old wreck," he snorted. "Who does that belong to?"

"It's team Hippo's. I'm fixing it up," replied Jace.

"Really? Well, good luck," replied the man, and he threw the black rubbish bag straight at Jace. Then he turned and stormed off.

Jace shook his head, astonished to see a grown-up, let alone a racing driver, behave like that.

He picked up the black bag and carried it over to the correct bin.

Then he went back to the Dexybel.

He couldn't afford any more interruptions.

The clock was ticking.

Chapter Three

Jace lifted the curved Dexybel bonnet.

"OK. I can do this…"

"Not unless you get on with it and stop talking to yourself," said a voice.

Jace turned, startled.

It was the little tablet computer! It had followed him, still hooked onto the trolley bin. Now it was sitting behind him with its lights blinking.

"Hurry up, Jace Tanna. Time to start."

"I was just about to," said Jace. "Listen, I don't want to be rude but I haven't got time

to talk…"

"Poor Jace Tanna.
No time."

There was a sudden buzzing sound and a cable unwound from the front of the tablet and curled onto the ground like a shoe-lace.

"Plug cable into vehicle. CherryPip will help."

Jace blinked.

"I don't think…"

"Plug cable into vehicle, Jace Tanna. CherryPip will check for faults. Quickest way."

Frowning, Jace took the end of the cable and looked for a connector on the Dexybel's dashboard. He found it beside the steering wheel and snapped the cable into place.

Buzzzz!

"Connection made..."

A row of green lights on the front of the tablet began flickering.

"...test beginning, please wait...no interruptions..."

Jace scratched his head. Surely this wouldn't work? The tablet – the CherryPip? – was only a waste removal control unit, not a machine specialist.

Jace glanced around the workshop, suddenly embarrassed in case any of the fixers had noticed what he was doing. Even worse, what if Maya happened to come past? Jace felt his face grow hot.

CLICK – BUZZZ!

"Faults found," announced the tablet suddenly. *"Test complete."*

"OK, then," whispered Jace. "Tell me. What did you find?"

"There's no electricity going from the batteries to the motor," the CherryPip reported immediately. *"Due to broken wires."*

"That doesn't sound good. What about the brakes?"

"The brake pedal is loose," the CherryPip said. *"Due to one missing bolt."*

"One bolt?" Jace scratched his head – if the problem was only a single bolt, maybe the brakes would not be too hard to fix after all…

"Thanks, CherryPip. Er – is there anything else?"

"Yes, Jace Tanna. Lots..."

CherryPip listed a string of problems, then blinked its lights at Jace.

"The car is worn out. Better to make another one."

"I can't. I've got to make this one work!"

"Start now then. Not much time."

The first problem was weight. The car was heavy and Jace needed to lift it, so he could work underneath it.

He asked two friendly fixers (bodywork experts) to help him push the vehicle onto the mag-lev lift.

The lift worked using magnetic levitation – the force of powerful electromagnets pushing away from each other – and it looked like magic.

When Jace pressed a button the mash-up machine rose slowly into the air. Then it stopped at just the right height, at the two-metre mark (Jace was 1 metre and 54 centimetres tall).

So far, so good.

Jace stepped underneath and looked up.

"OK – let's see if you were right, CherryPip…"

CherryPip *was* right.

Jace could see two electric wires flapping about not connecting anything. And the bolt that should be holding the brake pedal had

disappeared.

One by one, he checked-off the problems that CherryPip had told him about. He used a notebook to list the new parts that he would need.

Then he looked up at the battered blue machine and whispered: "Don't worry. You will race again, I promise."

He stepped back and pressed the maglev lift button.

He was starting to feel more hopeful. Maybe he really *could* do it – perhaps it would be possible to get the Dexy fixed in time.

But as the machine floated gently to the ground, Jace had a strange feeling, as though somebody was staring at him…

Chapter Four

Jace turned. Standing in the workshop doorway was a girl and a woman. They were wearing light blue racing overalls and holding crash helmets.

They couldn't
come any closer, because
drivers weren't allowed into the
workshop (and Mr Murcan would
soon spot anyone who tried).

It only took Jace a moment to realise
that they must be the Team Hippo crew:
the driver and navigator.

They were talking to Maya.

The girl was suprisingly young – in fact
she looked no older than Jace himself.

She was frowning anxiously, twisting a
finger through her curly hair.

The woman also looked worried. She was
saying something to Maya.

All three of them looked up at the clock
on the workshop's back wall.

Jace glanced up at it too.

The red numbers always showed the time left until the next race – and there wasn't much.

...RACE COUNTDOWN: 38 hours, 26 minutes, 22 seconds...

Maya said something to the driver, pointing towards Jace, and the woman smiled and nodded.

The girl smiled too. She looked at Jace and did a thumbs-up sign.

Jace nodded and then gave a thumbs-up back.

They were trusting him to do the job, and

to get it finished in time for the race.

A moment later they were gone and Maya was striding back up to her office.

Now more than ever Jace was determined to fix the Dexy.

At the end of the day, Jace dashed up the steps to Maya's office, with his notebook.

"OK. What parts do you need?" asked Maya.

"I've made a list."

He handed it over and Maya read through it.

"Two power connectors…a brake bolt…a fuse set…"

She opened her laptop.

"OK, let's see what they've got at my favourite scrap yard…"

She typed and hit send.

A message immediately pinged back. She smiled.

"Ah! They never let me down – best recyclers on the island!"

She beamed at him.

"It seems you're in luck, J. They've got all the parts. A delivery drone will be here first thing in the morning."

"Great! Thanks."

"Now," she smiled. "You'd best wash up and get home. Early start tomorrow, eh?"

Jace sprinted up the path away from the workshop. He couldn't wait to tell his mum about his amazing day.

He knew she would be as excited as he was.

And tomorrow – if he did his job right – he would see the Dexybel in action.

As he ducked through the bushes and along his favourite shortcut he pictured the blue racer roaring into life and being driven out onto the test track.

For one happy moment he even imagined that the Dexy could win the race.

But then he laughed and shook his head. It would be wonderful enough just to get it working.

He sprinted all the way home, past the

fenced-off building where Mr Murcan planned the race obstacles, then over the footbridge that crossed the race track (where you could stand for a great view if you knew how to get there!) and on into the woods.* He ran the whole way without stopping once, thinking about the Dexy spinning around the track.

Tomorrow was going to be the most exciting day of his life!

* *Find Jace's way home on the map at the start of this book.*

Chapter Five

The next morning dawned sunny and bright. By eight o'clock, Jace was standing outside the workshop looking at the clear blue sky.

But there was no sign of the delivery drone.

Come on! Fly faster, wherever you are…

He needed to start on the repairs.

He stared up at the sky – still nothing.

Everyone else was already hard at work – the repair teams in the workshop, the crews outside checking the track…

There was a flash of silver-blue as two Emergency Rescuers shot past on a

hoverbike, racing to get somewhere fast.

Only Jace himself seemed to be doing nothing.

He stared down the road.

There was no sign of the drone, only a man hurrying along muttering to himself. It was a moment before Jace recognised him. It was that racing driver from yesterday, the one with the rubbish bag…Deesol something or other…?

"Hmph! Bad person!" said a voice suddenly.

Jace turned. The little tablet computer was blinking up at him. It was still attached to its recycling bin.

"Oh, hello CherryPip – I was just waiting

Mash Track facts!

The new Model 4 now being used by the Rescuers is almost twice as fast as the old Model 3

New – extra storage space for tools and spares

Medical supplies compartment (all Rescuers are qualified first aiders)

Power booster

Air sucked in here

Improved twin air jets deliver more upwards lift

The Model 4 Hoverbike

for my delivery drone to arrive…"

"No point. Drone not coming. Follow me. Fast, fast!"

Jace ran after the little tablet as it wheeled across the car park with its trolley bin rattling. A piece of cardboard dropped out and Jace picked it up.

"Wait! Stop – where are you going?"

CherryPip ignored him and raced on. *"Delivery drone has crashed."*

"Crashed? How can it have crashed?"

"Rotor blade failure... cause unknown... hurry..."

As they reached the end of the car park Jace suddenly saw it – a heap of wreckage lying on the ground.

Bits of the broken drone were scattered everywhere.

And there was a package with his name on it, lying on top of the heap. It was torn and dented.

"Check for damage, Jace Tanna."

Jace did. He tore off the wrapping,

dreading what he'd find inside. *Please…*
please…

He lifted out the pieces, one at a time, as
CherryPip watched.

"It all seems OK…"

"You are lucky if no damage to parts."

"Phew!"

"But no time to talk. Hurry! Load
everything into trolley bin!"

"OK, good idea."

Jace loaded all the parts, carefully stacking them into the bin.

Then CherryPip wheeled at full speed, rattling across the car park.

The little tablet stopped outside the workshop entrance.

"CherryPip has work to do... CherryPip will get into trouble..."

"Right, don't worry. I can carry everything from here."

Jace unloaded the parts.

"And thanks for you help."

He watched as the little tablet trundled away.

As Jace was bringing in the spare parts, making a neat pile beside the Dexy, he noticed two figures standing in the shadows beneath Maya's office.

They were trying to keep their voices down – half whispering – but were having a disagreement about something.

And then Jace heard one of them mention his own name…

"…but isn't he a bit too young to be working here?…"

"…don't worry, I'm keeping an eye on him…"

"…but really! He'll never get that blue wreck working…"

"…it's tricky, I agree. But he's got a chance…I want to let him try…"

"…yes, yes, he can try. But trust me, that

machine won't even make it once around the test track…"

The conversation ended and Jace ducked behind the Dexy.

As he did, the bumper came loose in his hand.

Jace held his breath as one of the figures stalked away. He peeped and saw that it was Deesol Dragg. The other figure turned and climbed the metal steps. Maya was heading back up to her office.

...RACE COUNTDOWN: 19 hours ...

Now Jace had everything he needed, except time – the race would start the very next day.

And this was going to be a big job – so big, in fact, that most people wouldn't have bothered. They would have walked away and said that the old Dexy just wasn't worth fixing.

But Jace was different. He turned to the smashed up machine and started working.

A while later, just as Jace had finished fixing the fuses and was fitting the new brake bolt, Maya came by. She looked over his shoulder and smiled.

"Well done, J. You're doing great. By the time you're finished this Dexybel will be as good as the great Merlingo itself."

Jace looked at her.

"Merlingo?"

She nodded.

"Yes. The best machine ever to win here. When I was your age I had pictures of the Merlingo all over my bedroom wall. It won five times."

"Five times!" Jace's jaw dropped. "It must have been amazing."

"Yes, it was the fastest racer ever made," Maya replied. "But you know, when it first arrived on the island it was pretty beaten-up. Just like your Dexy here."

Jace wanted to know more but a fixer

called her away, over to the other side of the workshop.

...RACE COUNTDOWN: 15 hours, 4 minutes...

Just one thing left to do, thought Jace, wiping his hands on a cloth.

The repairs were all done, but now he had an extra idea. He looked up at Maya's office and hesitated. There was something he really wanted to ask her. But suddenly he felt unsure.

It might just sound crazy...

"Well? What is it?" Maya smiled.

Jace was standing nervously in the doorway.

"The repairs are done but…I want to make the Dexy go even faster."

She raised an eyebrow.

"And how are you going to do that?"

"Well, I've been thinking," said Jace. "Over in the workshop I saw some of those Super Ti-Ger battery packs. They're light-weight and extra energised. I think they'd fit in the Dexybel nicely…"

Maya chuckled.

"Extra energised, eh? I think you really *might* turn your Dexybel into a Merlingo!"

Jace laughed.

"I bet those batteries would boost the top speed. What do you think?"

"Maybe…" nodded Maya, impressed.

She thought about it for a moment.

"OK. But you'll have to fit them yourself. And you're running out of time" – she glanced at the clock – "we need to do the test drive tonight."

Jace stared, not sure if he'd heard correctly.

"*We* need to do the test drive?"

"Of course, J! You're coming with me. It's time you had a go on the track…"

Chapter Six

"Ready J?"

"Ready Maya!"

Jace was in the navigator's seat next to Maya, pulling his helmet over his head.

He'd fitted the Ti-Ger batteries in time and now the Dexy was ready for its test drive.

"Buckle up," said the chief fixer, and Jace snapped on his safety harness.

He couldn't quite believe it. He was about to get his very first ride around a race-track!

Maya pushed the starter button and the car burst into life. The electric motor – powered by its new Ti-Ger packs – spun like

never before.

Maya steered the
Dexybel out of the workshop,
along the pit lane and onto the
track.

"Nervous?" grinned Maya.

Jace shook his head – but his hands were
gripping tight to the sides of his seat.

Then Maya put her foot down on the
accelerator.

The Dexybel roared into life. Jace felt
himself being pressed back into his seat –
wwwwooooooaaaahh!! – and the machine flew
onto the circuit.

The Dexybel was much faster than Jace had expected.

His feet tingled and he felt a thrill in his stomach.

"Nice," shouted Maya. "Not just fast but stable too. Great handling!"

As they went into the first bend the Dexy was holding firmly onto the track surface.

Jace clutched his seat.

They came into the straight again, then

roared into one, two, three fast laps.

Suddenly something appeared, popping up in the road ahead.

"Hang on!" shouted Maya. "Here comes one of Mr Murcan's traps."

The traps! Jace knew about them of course, he'd seen them in videos.

They could appear anywhere – hidden tunnels, or sudden rock falls (with "safe" artificial rocks), or roaring rivers that appeared out of nowhere – but Jace had never experienced one of the traps for himself.

Until now.

Now he could see the obstacle rushing towards them, and it looked terrifying – a huge ramp, jutting upwards!

"Wooaaah!" shouted Jace.

Less than a second later they hit it –
KERTHUD – and his stomach lurched as
the Dexy flew up into the air.

For one, two, three, heart-stopping
seconds they flew. The Dexy roared and its
wheels spun against nothing.

Then it came down again with a bouncing
thud and its tyres gripped the track.

"Wow!" shouted Maya. "This machine
isn't just racing – it's flying! Mr Murcan will
have to do better than that if he wants to
stop your Dexy."

Jace was grinning with sheer delight.

Maya glanced at Jace – "Look out, I'm
going to try the brakes."

And she pressed the pedal hard.

Jace felt the harness straps bite into his shoulders. His eyes bulged and his ears popped. The Dexybel skidded to a halt. The tyres screeched in a cloud of smoke.

"Super cool!" shouted Maya. "You've done a fantastic job."

"Thanks," gasped Jace, feeling happier than he could ever remember.

He'd done it!

He'd fixed the mash-up machine in time.

Maya steered the Dexy back to the pit lane and, as she did, she nodded her head.

"Look, Jace."

Two figures were standing beside the track. The woman and the girl – Team Hippo's

driver and navigator in their light blue racing suits had been watching the test.

Not just watching, but cheering.

They were now jumping up and down, hugging each other, obviously delighted at how fast their beaten-up machine was going.

Jace gave a big thumbs-up as they drove past. The girl smiled and waved.

But neither of them noticed that somebody else was watching too.

The figure of a man was standing in the shadows next to the stands, with his arms folded. He had been studying the Dexybel closely.

As Maya and Jace drove past, one of his fists clenched in its expensive, new white glove.

Chapter Seven

The first race was about to begin.

Crowds began pouring in at dawn, buzzing with anticipation.

Everyone had their favourite teams and favourite drivers.

Jace arrived early and made his way through the crowds. He was desperate to find a good place to stand but he was surprised how hard it was. There were so many people already here, and all the best spots seemed to be taken.

Then he heard someone calling his name.

"Jace! Over here!"

It was Maya, waving and smiling broadly.

"I've got something for you," she said. "Don't lose it J, it's worth more than gold."

She put something in his hand – something small and flat – but before he had time to look and see what it was she was pointing towards the starting line.

"No time to talk" she said. "The race is about to start."

She hurried off – but glanced back at him as she went.

"See you in the pit stop, five minutes!" she

gestured.

Jace was about to call after her – "I'm not allowed in the pits."

Then he looked down at the thing in his hand. And he realised that, actually, he was!

The golden badge with its black and purple writing was unmistakable. What Maya had just given him was nothing less than an All-Areas Pass.

With one of those he could now go anywhere on the race circuit – even out onto the track.

His heart was pounding as he looped the purple ribbon over his head and felt the badge resting against his chest.

Wait till I tell everyone about this – they'll never believe it!

It almost made Jace wish that school was starting again soon, just so he could tell his friends. (Almost, but not quite).

Jace walked around the pits with care. Black cables as thick as pythons had been laid across the ground by the news crews covering the event. The Mash-Up Machines Challenge was being filmed so the fans could see all the action.

Suddenly Jace wondered whether some of his school friends might actually catch a glimpse of him in the news – because now he was going to be right where all the action started.

He glanced up at the enormous screen

towering over the stands.

When the race started the screen would show the action, close-up – and if you wore the special glasses, you'd see it all in 3D! Jace had a pair in his pocket.

But right now, before the start, the crews were being interviewed.

Jace stopped.

Up on the screen were two faces that he recognised.

"…and here we have Ashley and Lexie, Team Hippo's driver and navigator…" the commentator was saying "…tell me, is your hippopotamus very fast?…"

Jace grinned. Ashley and Lexie – that's what his teammates were called…

"…we call it the Dexybel…" Lexie was

saying. "…and wow, it's quick – very – all thanks to a brilliant fixer here at the track…"

"…fantastic!…" said the commentator.

"…his name is Jace Tanna and he's super cool…" added driver Ash, with a thumbs-up to the camera.

Jace felt his face grow hot and looked down, hoping that nobody would spot him after all.

As Jace approached the pits, the security guard at the gates smiled and immediately unlocked them. Visitors and fans were never allowed in here – but, thanks to his All-Areas Pass, Jace was.

Now he found himself inside.

He made his way down the pit lane, past the garages, each one with the name of a race team painted above the doors.

Svenja Masher…Curlew Capri…Zonka Speedkings… Hakondi Hackers…Team Dragg…

Peering into each garage as he passed, Jace could see the crews climbing into their machines.

"OUCH!"

Suddenly Jace tripped and sprawled onto the ground.

"Look where you're going!"

"S…sorry," gasped Jace, scrambling to his feet.

His heart jumped – it was that driver again, Deesol Dragg.

"Are you OK?"

"You shouldn't be here, this area is for important people only –"

The man brushed some invisble dirt from his sleeve. Suddenly, he stopped. He was staring at the pass around Jace's neck. "Where did you get that?"

"I was given it…"

For a moment Deesol Dragg frowned,

but just as quickly he brightened, pointing at Jace.

"I know *you*. You're the boy who fixed Team Hippo's brakes in record time."

Jace nodded.

"Well done!" beamed the driver, clapping his white glove on Jace's shoulder. "Who would have thought it, eh? Beginner's luck probably."

He smiled and his moustache spread out like a caterpillar having a stretch.

"You know me already, of course," continued the man. "I'm Deesol Dragg, the famous racing driver."

He sighed. "I suppose you want my autograph?"

He stuck his hand in his pocket and began

fumbling for a pen. But at that moment a siren sounded, making him jump.

MESSAGE TO ALL DRIVERS! ALL DRIVERS! PLEASE START YOUR ENGINES!

"Sorry, no time," snapped Dragg.

And he was gone, dashing off towards his racer.

"Jace! Time to leave the pits," called a voice.

Jace turned and there was Maya, striding towards him, smiling broadly.

"Come on, this place is about to fill with

racers. Let's get up to the starting line. We'll get the best view there."

"OK – coming!"

Jace ran after Maya towards the stands. Ahead, the crowd was buzzing with excitement.

Thousands of flags were being waved and the air shook with cheers. Amid all the noise Jace thought he could hear people shouting – 'Hip-po! Hip-po! Hip-po!" – and he began to join in.

Then he spotted Deesol Dragg again, climbing into his racer. Deesol's machine was the Zodium. It was very smart, with no dents or scratches. Jace stared at it. It looked brand new, hardly like a mash-up machine at all. It also looked fiercely fast.

Jace blinked – Deesol suddenly looked pretty fierce too.

The famous racing driver seemed to be having a problem with his navigator.

The navigator was a large man with a chunky, square-shaped head. He was having difficulty squeezing his helmet onto it.

He shook his head from side to side. The helmet was hurting his ears.

"For goodness sake, Thud, get *IN*!" Deesol was ordering through gritted teeth – all the while trying to keep his smile in place for the watching cameras.

And at that moment the racers came out, crunching onto the track.

They all looked great. The Zodium,
the Suzonda, the Yamanix, the Mamoote.
And especially, thought Jace, the little blue
Dexybel.

He cheered as it came into view.

It still looked scrappy – but now, as it

rolled forward, and its bodywork flashed in the sun, those dents didn't make it look worn-out any more.

They made it look hardy.

Rumble...rumble...

J

Jace straightened up with pride as Ash and Lexie rumbled past and he saw them waving to the crowds through the open window.

Yes, the Dexbel now looked like what it really was: a tough survivor – a mash-up machine ready to give its all.

Chapter Eight

The sight of the mash-up machines getting ready to go was one of the most thrilling things Jace had ever seen.

Engines revved, the ground shook and the crowd cheered.

"It gets more exciting every year!" shouted Maya.

Now the racers were lining up on the grid, two by two, all revving like mad.

Team Hippo's Dexybel was about half-way up the line and Jace stood on tip-toes to wave.

Then, right at the front, he spotted Deesol Dragg.

103

Somehow Dragg
had managed to weave
his Zodium in and out, and
force his way to the lead position
for the start.

"How did he do that?" gasped Jace.
But Maya didn't hear him.

"Look!" she called, nudging his arm.
"It's Mr Lobb – he has to start the race."

Mr Lobb was the V.I.P. (or Very
Important Person) who always had to start
the race.

He loved the Fantastic Electric Mash-
Up Track (which he owned) and he loved
the machines – but he didn't like being the

official race starter. He was shy and timid, and that made him quite the wrong person for the job.

But Mr Murcan insisted, saying that it would not be proper for anyone else to do it.

"It has to be you."

Now, as Mr Lobb stepped up onto the podium – prodded forward by Mr Murcan – he was whispering to himself.

"Lift, wave, drop…lift, wave, drop…"

That's all he had to do: lift the flag above his head (the big flag with the black-and-white squares), wave it… and let it drop.

When the flag dropped, the race would begin.

Easy.

"Lift, wave, drop…" Mr Lobb repeated to

himself. "Lift, wave…"

…and he glanced at the first car.

Unfortunately he looked straight into the eyes of Deesol Dragg. Those eyes glared back at him. And beneath the eyes a furious moustache was twitching.

"Get on with it!" Deesol yelled.

And Mr Lobb jumped, fumbled – and the flag went flying.

Deesol took off like a rocket, way ahead of the other racers. A huge roar went up from the crowd as the others followed.

The first race was underway.

"Did you see what he did?" Jace shouted to Maya, above the cheers.

"Who? Did what?"

"Deesol Dragg! He cheated!"

But Maya
didn't hear him.
The chief fixer was
too busy punching
the air, cheering after the
last of the machines as they
sped away. Her eyes were
wide with excitement.

"Mmm?" she smiled. "What did you say?"

And Jace found that he couldn't repeat the words. They sounded all wrong –

107

saying them had made him feel like a spoilt
child who didn't like losing.

"Oh, nothing…"

Maya slapped him on the back.

"Great start for your Dexybel, eh?
Fantastic!"

And Jace saw that Maya was right.

Team Hippo had surged forward,
overtaking machine after machine. Driver
Ash and navigator Lexie were already
pushing towards the group at the front.

Deesol Dragg called himself The Famous
Racing Driver, not because he was, but
because that's what he wanted to be. Famous.

Whooooosh!

But now, as he roared along the amazing Mash-Up Track in lead position, he had an even better idea. He began chuckling to himself.

"A new name…Deesol Dragg, The Famous CHAMPION Racing Driver – hmmm… or how about Deesol Dragg, The Famous CHAMPION WINNING Racing Driver – not bad…"

He looked at his navigator.

"Hey! What do you think of my new

name, Thudd?"

"New name? Uh? Aren't you Deesol Dragg any more?"

Thudd tried to turn his head, but his helmet was wedged.

"Of course I am, you idiot! But I'm now the Famous CHAMPION WINNING

Racing Driver…"

Thudd didn't know what to say, so he nodded – or tried to – and the too-tight

Screeeechh!

straps on his helmet made his ears flap.

Dragg's smile vanished as a racer appeared in his mirror and began edging towards him.

He thrust his foot hard on the accelerator pedal, and the purple Zodium surged forward again.

Jace and Maya – and the whole crowd – were watching all the action on the screens.

In the Dexybel, Ash and Lexie were storming ahead. They had passed a whole group of machines and were running five places behind Deesol Dragg and Thud.

Jace punched the air as Ash weaved around another racer (the Acceligator) to take fourth position.

Then suddenly, he became aware of somebody standing at his shoulder.

"Interesting…very interesting…"

It was Mr Murcan, studying the action on the big screen, his eyes narrowed.

Maya glanced round too.

"Oh, hi Mr M," she beamed cheerfully. "Pleased with the action?"

"Not bad so far," replied Mr Murcan. "Surprising…" he added, looking at Jace. "I didn't think the Dexybel was capable of such speed."

"That's because I…" began Jace – but before he could explain about the Ti-Ger batteries Maya nudged him in the ribs.

"That's because Jace greased the wheels," the chief fixer smiled.

Mr Murcan frowned.

"Hmmm. It must be very effective grease," he said.

"Oh yes, it is," said Maya, tapping the side of her nose. "Trade secret."

Then she leaned in close to Jace.

"No need to reveal all your tricks," she whispered.

A shout went up from the crowd.

One of Mr Murcan's traps had claimed its

Rumble...rumble...

first victims.

Without any warning, a spring-ramp had popped up just a few cars in front of the Dexybel, and two of the racers had bumped each other. The Curlew Capri

Zooooom!

and the Zonka Speedkings' machine, Orca-bomb, now flew out of control, spinning up clouds of dust.

Slamming left, Ash just about managed to avoid the ramp.

It was a skilful move, and at a stroke it put Team Hippo just two places behind the lead.

Mr Murcan nodded, satisfied, then turned and stalked away, vanishing into the crowd.

Maya chuckled.

"You know what he was doing?"

Jace shook his head.

"Mr Murcan never relaxes," explained Maya. "Did you see him studying the teams? He's already planning the next race. He'll be watching those cars and thinking about what obstacles to build."

Jace nodded. The obstacles – that's what everyone really wanted to see…

"Look! Here they come again!" shouted Maya suddenly.

And the air shook as the machines screamed past, completing their fourth lap.

Team Dragg was in the front. Team Hippo was now third.

The racer in second place suddenly lost speed.

Jace looked up at the screen, wondering what was happening.

Then he realised.

It was the Suzonda, a clever machine with solar panel boosters that gave it impressive extra speed. But this secret weapon now became its hidden weakness. Because one of the panels had somehow come loose and it was flapping about – like a broken feather hanging from a bird's wing – robbing the engine of its extra energy. The Suzonda slowed.

There was a groan from the stands. The racing fans winced, feeling sorry for the driver.

But there was nothing he could do to keep up top speed.

Ash took her chance – the Suzonda's back luck was her good fortune – and the Dexybel sailed past into second place.

Even with their crash helmets on, Ash and Lexie could hear the crowd cheer.

"Hip-po! Hip-po! Hip-po!"

And Ash pushed the little Dexy even harder.

Beside her, Lexie was concentrating on the map. She had spent hours getting ready for this, studying the way, learning every twist and bump.

And she knew how to give instructions.

"…left bend coming up… now another… brake hard… harder!… OK now… extreme

right bend ahead…
careful… CAREFUL! …
OK, go straight for
a long run. Go,
GOOOO!"

Ash didn't
say a word,
but she didn't
need to. She trusted

Rumble...Roaarrr!

Lexie completely. She was listening to
every instruction.

As the Dexybel passed the stands again,
towards the final lap, only Team Dragg's
Zodium was still ahead.

"We've got them," shouted Lexie, her
eyes flashing. "We can do this! We can
win!"

120

Ash pressed her foot hard to the floor, and the Dexybel surged on.

Thudd was doing his best. The thing is, he didn't really want to be a navigator and he didn't know much about maps.

Which is why he was holding the track map upside down.

This meant that every time he warned Deesol about a left turn ahead, a right turn suddenly appeared instead – which was unfortunate.

"Uuuuurgggghhh!" screamed Deesol Dragg.

He tugged frantically on the steering wheel, narrowly avoiding another crash.

"Careful, you idiot!"

After a while, Dragg worked out what was happening.

He glared at Thudd, his mouth twitching – but for once he didn't say anything. He decided the easiest solution would be if he just did the opposite of everything that Thudd told him.

So from now on, when Thudd said left, Dragg would go right.

"That'll fix it," he muttered.

And it would have – except that Thudd had also realised his silly mistake. So now he turned the map the right way up.

"Left ahead Boss…that's it left… left… NO LEFT!"

"Uuuuurgggghhh!"

And the Zodium nearly crashed again.

As they entered the final lap they were in the lead position still, but only just. The Dexybel was close. So close its bumper was almost touching the Zodium.

And the tough little machine was about to shoot past.

The crowd was going wild.

Up on the screens they could see the two race leaders were now screeching along side by side.

The Zodium and the Dexybel were locked in battle.

And in the Dexybel, Team Hippo was starting to edge ahead.

The scrappy blue racer was beating the flashy purple one – it seemed impossible.

"Hip-po! Hip-po! Hip-po!"

Maya put her arm around Jace.

"Well done! You've worked wonders!"

And then, without any warning, across

the screens went blank. For the first time ever in the Mash-Up Championship's history, the video link failed.

A confused chatter rose up from the

stands – a wave of disappointment – and a strange silence fell.

It seemed as if everyone was holding their breath, waiting for the picture to come back on. The silence seemed to last for ages – then suddenly, somebody shouted:

"Here they come! Here come the winners!"

Everybody jumped to their feet as the leading machines tore around the final corner and careered down the home straight towards the finish.

Jace jumped onto his seat, cheering and trying to see.

"Did they do it?" he shouted. "Did Hippo come first?!"

Maya turned – and for once she wasn't

smiling.

"The Zodium won. And there's no sign of the Dexybel. They must have crashed out."

Chapter Nine

Ash and Lexie had crashed. The Dexybel was now lying on its side in a tangle of grass and rocks beside the track.

A team of Rescuers arrived at the spot within seconds, the blue lights flashing on their hoverbikes. The rescue operation was fast and efficient.

A while later, Jace watched it all replay three or four times on the screen outside the workshop.

…Ash and Lexie were helped away from the wreckage… they were shaken, but

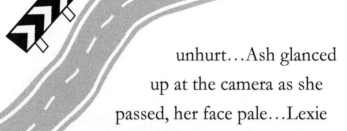

unhurt…Ash glanced up at the camera as she passed, her face pale…Lexie turned away…

Then the picture cut to endless action replay shots of the Zodium shooting over the winning line, and close-ups of Deesol Dragg waving triumphantly to the crowd.

Jace was now alone.

Maya had given him a consoling hug – "you did great – the Dexy was fantastic" – then she hurried off to supervise the Rescuers.

The other cars were already rolling back in

– the CC Racing 8686, the Svenja, the solar Suzonda. Twenty four vehicles had made it, six had been knocked out. Including the Dexybel.

Lexie came striding over, her racing helmet under her arm.

"I wanted to say thanks," she said, grim faced. "You did a great job with our Dexy."

She held out her hand.

"I'm Lexie."

"Hi, I'm Jace."

Then she leaned close and whispered: "They cheated, I know they did."

Jace looked at her.

"You mean Dragg?"

"Yes. I'm pretty sure they dumped oil on the track, or something like that. We hit a slippery patch. It was like driving on ice."

"I knew it," nodded Jace. "You and Ash were driving so well. And there's something else – I think Dragg cheated at the start."

Lexie clenched her fists.

"Really?"

"Yes. I was the only one who spotted it but…"

Jace was about to say more but just then Maya appeared, with Ash and a group of other drivers and fixers.

"Come on you two," she said. "The after-race meeting is about to start."

Mr Murcan stood at the podium.

He tapped the microphone – POP, POP – then scanned the room, as the race teams and officials took their seats. Ash, Lexie and Jace squeezed in at the back.

Chairs scraped. The air was filled with

excited chatter.

"Quickly now. We've got a lot to get through… I know you're all excited…"

And then hush descended and Mr Murcan began. He read out the names of the winning teams, and their times.

"…everyone did well, but only twenty teams can go through to the next race…so… the successful teams are…in first place, Team Dragg…1 hour, 13 minutes, 22.2 seconds… in second place Svenja Masher…1 hour, 14 minutes, 9.7 seconds…in third place…"

And the list went on, spoken softly and relentlessly.

It was as if Mr Murcan was chanting a terrible spell – that had the power to make some people unbelievably happy, and others beyond-words sad.

It was the worst afternoon of Jace's life.

Even as he sat there, a small part of him hoped that Team Hippo's name would somehow be included among the winners.

Beside him, Lexie was sitting frozen, her face still and grim, as if she was made of stone.

"…and now, my deepest commiserations to the teams who will not being going through…"

But then a hand was raised and Mr Murcan paused. He frowned.

"…can't it wait?…"

"…Excuse me…"

Maya stood, smiling – "…whoops…" – as her seat bumped the person behind. "Sorry to interrupt you, Mr M, but I think you've forgotten about Team Hippo."

"You are mistaken," replied Mr Murcan. "Team Hippo is on my list. If you will be patient, I am about to confirm which teams have been eliminated."

"But surely Team Hippo will be going through?"

Lexie and Jace glanced at each other.

Maya was holding something up in her hand – a small black book.

"According to the Mash-Up Championship rules – er, here it is, rule three – "any team which breaks a lap-speed record in any race is automatically a winner". Hippo did break a lap-speed record, not just once but three times – in laps two, six and seven. That's never been done before."

Mr Murcan's mouth opened, and for a few seconds he was speechless.

"One moment…"

Then he turned to his assistant. A group of race officials huddled round and began talking in urgent whispers.

And then Mr Murcan came back to the podium. His face was as calm as ever, and his voice as dry as if nothing had happened. But it had.

"…my apologies…I can confirm that
Team Hippo also qualifies for race two…"

He continued speaking but the rest of his

words were lost as a thunderous cheer went
up all around the room – among the winning
teams, and even the losers. Everyone was
clapping.

Only Deesol Dragg was scowling, but now not a single person in the room was paying him any attention.

Ash, Lexie and Jace stared at each other, mouths wide with astonishment – and then they were lost in a sea of hugs and backslapping.

"…settle down please…come on now, settle down…"

But for once Mr Murcan had no choice but to wait patiently as the whole room celebrated.

Chapter Ten

"The battle isn't over," said Maya grimly as Team Hippo (driver Ash, navigator Lexie and their new fixer, Jace) headed back to the workshop. "Your Dexybel is damaged massively and you've only got three days to make repairs."

"We'll do it," smiled Lexie, squeezing Jace's shoulders. "Our machines expert can do anything."

Maya shook her head. "He's good, but he's not a magician."

And as they reached the workshop – and

saw the wreck of the little racer for the first time – all of them realised that she was right.

"It's a disaster," breathed Ash, staring at the crumpled body and the shattered glass. "We'll never do it."

"I don't see how you can," agreed Maya. "Even if you could get all the spares, there's not enough time to fix them all together."

Ash looked from the Dexy to Jace and Lexie.

"It's sad," she sighed. "But it's still better than any of us dared to hope. We broke three speed records – Team Hippo did brilliantly. And next year we'll be back."

Maya nodded.

"That's the spirit."

But Jace wasn't ready to give in. Not yet. He scrambled over to his tool kit.

"There has to be a way! We've got to keep the Dexy flying!"

All his tools were there, and the CherryPip – the CherryPip! Of course! The little tablet had been watching them talk – now it wheeled forward with its bin, lights flashing.

Buzzz… its connector cable coiled out. Jace connected it to the Dexybel.

"What do we need CherryPip?"

The computer buzzed and clicked.

"Panels… chassis… steering column… brake cables… oh dear…what have you

been doing to it?"

"There was an accident. In the race."

"Yes, yes. I'm checking the race reports now. Please wait, Jace Tanna."

"Jace," said Lexie, coming to stand next to him. "I think Ash is right. We'll be back next year – and we definitely want you to be our fixer. You're the best."

"Wait Lexie – this might work…"

"Summoning drone…"

A passing drone suddenly diverted. It came buzzing down. It hovered over the Dexybel, then landed next to them. Its rotor blades stopped turning.

"Please connect CherryPip to the drone…"

"What? Why?"

"Please connect Cherrypip to the

drone..."

Jace sighed. He tugged the computer cable out from the car, then he plugged it into the drone.

"I don't see how this helps."

The drone buzzed into action again. It hovered beside the CherryPip, and to Jace's astonishment, its mechanical arms (the ones that usually carried vehicle parts) picked up the tablet.

"CherryPip is now mobile!"

Up it went, hovering around the Dexybel.

"What are you doing, CherryPip?"

"I told you before. This machine is worn out. Repair for next race is impossible."

And with that, it buzzed away, whizzing out through the workshop door.

Jace watched it go, speechless. He was about to call it back, but at that moment Deesol Dragg appeared.

"You ran a brilliant race, Team Hippo, well done!" he boomed generously, striding towards them.

Then he noticed the Dexybel. "Wow, that looks bad – awful! – it's a miracle nobody got hurt…but never mind that, I've got something to cheer you up."

He turned to Thudd, who was standing behind him.

"Come on, man, quick… give it to me… hurry up…"

Thudd fumbled in his pocket.

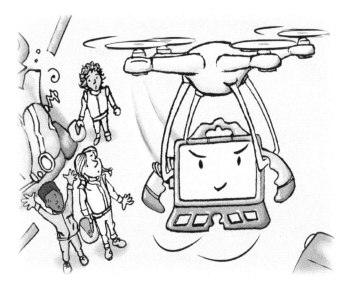

Then Dragg turned back and smiled at Jace.

"My dear boy. I remembered, see? I bet you thought I hadn't. You wanted my autograph!"

And he handed Jace a piece of paper.

"I may be famous," he chuckled modestly. "But I never forget my fans."

Jace stared at the paper in astonishment, but before he could say anything (he really didn't want the autograph) Dragg was striding off again.

Thudd went lumbering behind him.

Jace's shoulders slumped. The Dexy was broken. The CherryPip was gone. And Deesol Dragg was the winner.

Finally, even Jace had to admit it. Team Hippo was beaten.

Chapter Eleven

Three days later, the CherryPip came flying back. It was the morning of the second race.

It buzzed over the pit stops. It whizzed around the stands, where huge crowds were gathering. Then it landed in front of the workshop.

Jace was there, standing together with Lexie and Ash.

They'd been forced out of the championship, but they still wanted to be here for the start. Ash was now cheering for Team Solar – the driver was a good friend.

151

"They'd better watch
out for slippery patches,"
Lexie whispered to Jace.

The morning sun was shining, the sky
was blue and, finally, after two gloomy days,
Jace was feeling more cheerful. At least a bit.

"Winning this time doesn't matter,"
Maya had told him. "Everyone has
disappointments, you just have to pick
yourself up. What really matters is that
you've gone from sweeping the floor to
being a mash-up fixer. I'm going to make
you a full member of the team, just as I
promised. From now on, you can come back
every school holiday. If you want to…?"

And she looked at Jace with such a cheerful smile that Jace couldn't stop himself from smiling too.

Of course he wanted to come back! And of course Maya was right – sometimes you just have to pick yourself up.

ATTENTION! ALL TEAMS PREPARE YOUR MACHINES! RACE STARTING IN EIGHT MINUTES!

In the garages, fixers finished their last checks and drivers zipped up their overalls.

Mr Murcan appeared, leading Mr Lobb by the elbow towards the starting block.

"Lift, wave, drop…(and don't look at the drivers)…lift, wave, drop…(and don't look at the drivers)…" Mr Lobb was whispering to himself.

And then, the CherryPip flew in.

"Solution found."

The little tablet hovered in front of Jace, almost touching his nose.

"What?"

"Please adjust hearing. I said solution found."

"CherryPip, I don't know where you've been but…"

But his words were drowned out by the THWOK! THWOK! THWOK! of an approaching helicopter.

Rumble...rumble...

The helicopter was a powerful machine designed for lifting. A shipping container was suspended beneath it, swinging on cables. On the sides of the container were stamped bold, green letters:

MASH-UP CHAMPIONS MUSEUM – SPARES & REPAIRS

It was an amazing sight. A picture of it flashed onto the giant video screen. The race commentator's voice rose with excitement.

"What's going on here, ladies and gentlemen?…I don't think this is part of the programme today…there's never a dull moment here at Mash-Up racing, that's for sure!"

The helicopter was lowering the container gently to the ground. It landed right in front of the starting line.

"NO! NO! NO!" Mr Murcan was striding out onto the track, waving his arms.

By now the first racers were gathering on the starting line. Dragg's Zodium didn't need to push its way to the front this time. He was the race one winner so he would start in pole position, at the front, by right.

"Solution found," repeated the CherryPip, buzzing towards the helicopter.

"Come on," exclaimed Lexie. "Let's go and see!"

The helicopter's passenger door opened and a man in a brown coat struggled to climb out.

"What are you doing?" snapped Mr Murcan, striding across to confront him.

The man, who looked rather old and frail, turned and peered up at him through a thick pair of glasses.

"I'm sorry to interrupt," he said. "I'm the caretaker at the Mash-Up Champions Museum. I would have come sooner but my knees are a bit stiff…too many years sweeping… Umm, I understand you have a machine that needs repairing? It's called the Dexybel, I think?"

Mr Murcan tapped his watch.

"It's far too late. We start in five minutes."

"Well, we can't do anything in five minutes," replied the man, shaking his head. "Sorry, good machines can't be rushed. Except when they're racing – " (he paused to chuckle at his own joke) "But really, I have to disagree with you on that other point. It's never too late."

"Sir, you have to move this helicopter!"

And then a big argument broke out.

Two fixers and the pilot jumped out from the helicopter – then Ash, Lexie, Maya and Mr Lobb also ran onto the track – and Deesol Dragg came storming over too, with Mr Thudd lumbering behind him. Then the other race teams joined in, followed by the news crews, all shouting at once.

Jace felt a hand on his shoulder.

"Young man, could I have a word?" whispered a voice.

It was the caretaker – the old man in the brown overalls – he had squeezed out from the crowd and was beckoning to Jace. While the argument went on, they slipped away to the side of the track.

"We saw what a good job you did on that little Dexybel. Such a thrill seeing it in action – it's a shame about that accident. Very odd."

His eyes twinkled at Jace through the thick lenses.

"Anyway, we know Team Hippo can't do all those repairs, so we thought we'd do them *for* you. Everyone at the museum agrees. You deserve it."

"Thank you," replied Jace. "I don't know what to say."

"Don't say anything then, come on – let's get the Dexybel loaded. The sooner we start, the sooner you can have it back."

He turned, and headed back towards the

crowd, leaning on Jace's arm to keep himself steady.

"Oh, I nearly forgot," he said, stopping again. "Don't be downhearted. Have you ever heard the story of the famous Merlingo?"

"The Merlingo? The machine that won five times?"

"That's the one. It was a real champion, the Merlingo was. What a machine! Anyway, the thing is – " he pointed towards the container. "We thought you might like to use it."

The container door dropped open – CLANG! – and the Merlingo rolled forwards. An astonished silence fell over the track.

Nothing like this had ever happened before. Even the news commentator was lost for words.

The machine – the most brilliant red, gold and black – came out on auto-control. It drove slowly along in front of the stands, its engine whirring, and horn honking.

Then it flashed its lights and the crowd broke into a roar – louder, even, than when they cheered during the races.

Meanwhile, the fixers, the ones who had arrived in the helicopter, brought out a rescue-trolley, and gently started moving the wreckage of the Dexybel up to the container.

The red Merlingo cruised over and wheeled along beside it.

And almost, for a moment, it was as if

Rumble...rumble...

the two machines were talking to each other.

The Merlingo's headlights flashed and the signal reflected back brightly from Dexy's own lamps.

Then the red car turned, revved its engine, and rolled over to where Ash, Lexie and Jace were standing, too astonished to speak.

And they saw it.

The picture.

On the side of the Merlingo was a newly-painted hippo wearing a hat and sunglasses.

And there were letters beneath it, bold and cheerful:

"Watch out on the track –
The Hippo is back!"

"Well, if you've all quite finished," said Mr Murcan dryly, his hands clamped behind his back. "Please go to your places. It's time to

start the second race."

He looked at Ash and Lexie.

"And if you two plan to drive this machine, I suggest you get into it."

So that's exactly what they did.

Try this Mash-Up treasure hunt...

Turn to the map at the start of the book, and see if you can find:

[ ] A good place to get some pizza
[ ] Where the oldest trees on the island grow
[ ] The place where Mr Murcan gets his best view
[ ] A good sleeping place for bats

And finally, how many bridges can you spot?
[ ]1 [ ]2 or [ ]3 ?